Rock-A-Bye Snoopy

Can The Gang Help Snoopy Fall Asleep?

Based on the comic strip "Peanuts"
Created and Written by:
Charles M. Schulz

Produced and Directed by:
Lee Mendelson
Desirée Goyette

Original Music and Lyrics by:
Desirée Goyette

Music Arranged and Conducted by:
Ed Bogas

Art Director:
Frank Hill

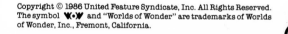

"Good Night, Me"

When I'm having trouble
   falling asleep
All those crazy thoughts
   from the busy day keep
Running around in
   my head
Keeping me from going
   to bed

I just close my eyes, the
   stars for my blanket
I relax my sleepy body
   and thank it
For being so true
Let me demonstrate
   to you…

Goodnight knees,
   goodnight paws
You deserve some special
   applause
For helping me to run
   and helping me to walk
And to pick a pretty daisy
   for Woodstock

Goodnight ears,
   goodnight eyes
Thanks for helping me
   see the sunrise
And children in the park,
   starlight when it's dark

And to listen to the song
   of the meadowlark

It's nice to know I've
   someone I can trust
To help me through every
   single day
I know they'll never leave
   me in the dust
No matter what I ask
   them to do they obey!

Goodnight stomach,
   you're pretty neat
Thanks for telling me
   when it's time to eat
A chocolate chip cookie
   with a little spot of tea
Or banana cream pie or
   cherries jubilee
Or a strawberry lemon tart
   or apple pie ala mode
Or a triple decker
sundae…

Hey I'm hungry!!

"Good Thoughts"

So you can't quite get
  to sleep
Even though you've
  counted a million sheep
Well here's my
  favorite plan
To take you off to
  dreamland…

Get rid of those
  bad thoughts, those
  sad thoughts
Those golly-gee makes
  you mad thoughts
Think of laughter and
  forget-me-nots
But don't get caught with
  a bad thought

Sleepytime's no time
  to pout
Keep the good thoughts in
Kick the bad thoughts out
Just relax get rid of
  your doubt
'Cause that's what
  sleepin's about

Fill your head with all of
  life's wonderful things
Like gingerbread
And butterfly wings
And how beautifully
  Woodstock sings

Or the puzzle you did
And how good it felt
  when every piece fit
Or the home run I once hit
Just pick up any doubt
  and throw it
You'll be asleep before
  you know it

C'mon and practice those
  good thoughts
Robin Hood thoughts
Movie star in Hollywood
  thoughts
Try to do as you've
  been taught
Now's the time to give it
  all I've got
Sleepytime's comin'
  ready or not
Just keep thinkin' those
  good thoughts

"Rock-A-Bye Baby"

Rock-a-bye baby on the tree top
When the wind blows the cradle
   will rock
When the bough breaks the cradle
   will fall
And down will come baby cradle
   and all

Rock, rock, rock-a-bye baby
On that little tree top
Take your little baby and swing
   her around
And go rockin' all around the clock
We're gonna rock and roll 'til we
   lose control
We're gonna hop 'n bop and we ain't
   never gonna stop
Gonna rock, rock, rock-a-bye baby
On that ever-lovin' tree top

"Bunny Wunnies"

How do bunny wunnies fall asleep?
They don't waste their time counting sheep
They climb into bed all in a row
And momma bunny wunnie sings to them like so…

Goodnight bunny wunnies
Mornin' comes soon

Sleep tight bunny wunnies
Under the moon

All the stars above
A vigil keep

Goodnight bunny wunnies
Go to sleep

Goodnight bunny wunnies
Mornin' comes soon

Sleep tight bunny wunnies
Under the moon

All the stars above
A vigil keep

Goodnight bunny wunnies
Go to sleep

Goodnight bunny wunnies
Go to sleep

THE
END